# POISONED CANDY

## BITE-SIZED HORROR

A collection of Halloween Horror
By Pippa Bailey and Myk Pilgrim



PUGNACIOUS PRESS

First published in Great Britain in 2018 by Pugnacious Press.



Kindly edited by Linda Nagle

Cover design and book art by Myk Pilgrim,
using elements under a Creative Commons 4.0 licence and gin.

Book formatting, admin, marketing,
and Pilgrim wrangling by Pippa Bailey.

www.pugnaciouspress.com

www.patreon.com/pugnaciouspress

# TRIGGER WARNING

Pilgrim here. Firstly, we wanted to say a big 'ol thank you for picking up this book.
Well, that, and give you a heads-up or two.

Pippa and I (being a skeezy, scummy, vulgar pair) have spared no "expense" in the taste department for Poisoned Candy.
Be warned, folks: the dog dies, the children seldom (if ever) outrun the monster, and mommy and daddy aren't here to protect you from the thing in the closet - in fact, mommy and daddy make the monsters look like toothless puppies.
All in "drabble" form --that means 100 words, no more, no less.

This book touches on sensitive issues such as degenerative diseases, murder, bullying, necrophilia, coprophagia, copious quantities of vomit, bodily fluids,
—which, let's be honest here, shall we, are all pretty much the same thing.
The publishers advise readers to proceed with caution; you have been warned.

Hello, publishers here again, consider this a second warning.
There's some tasteless shit in this book.
If you read on and get upset,
that is very much your fault.

RANCID EGGS
BITE-SIZED HORROR
PIPPA BAILEY & MYK PILGRIM

DEVIL'S NIGHT
BITE-SIZED HORROR
PIPPA BAILEY & MYK PILGRIM

POISONED CANDY
BITE-SIZED HORROR
PIPPA BAILEY & MYK PILGRIM

THE LITTLE BOOK OF
HARM
VERONICA ABBOTT

A SZIMPLA ÖRÖMET OKOZHAT!
THE DIVE

More titles available from

PUGNACIOUS PRESS

Purveyors of the Weird & Unusual.

Publishers of Peculiar Horror.

Devil's Night: Bite-Sized Horror for Halloween

Rancid Eggs: Bite-sized Horror for Easter

Bloody Stockings: Bite-sized Horror for Christmas

Poisoned Candy: Bite-sized Horror for Halloween

The Little Book of Harm

**www.pugnaciouspress.com**

# PUGNACIOUS PRESS

This book was created with the fine contributions of our excellent Patrons.

J.W. Donely

Katie Whittle

Mark Young

Nelson W. Pyles

If you would also like to get access to years and years of private notebooks from our indentured authors, listen in on story brainstorming sessions, behind the scenes video diaries, research notes, get copies of books in advance of public release AND see your name in print –

Then you need to haul ass over to the Pugnacious Press Patreon page at

**https://www.patreon.com/pugnaciouspress**

and be blown away by how much awesome you can get for one measly dollar a month.

*Thank you cider, we couldn't have done this without you.*

*Well, we could have,*
*but fuck, it would have been a lot less fun.*

## Halloween Love

Candles mounted on the gravestone above lend a supernatural splendour to the starlit October night.

Josie's overdue kisses are intense, their tremors rippling through her frame in localised earthquakes. The picnic scattered around them on the grass has gone untouched, again.

Josie straddles her Evan, the sensation of his bare skin against hers shortens her breath, making her shudder.

When she comes, it's Niagara Falls.

Her heart still pounding a metal concert drum solo, she hoists him up and places him back into his coffin.

After one last peck on his dead cheek, she shovels back the cold, wet earth.

## Run, Winnie, Run!

Branches scratch at Winnie's wrinkled face as she sprints through the nocturnal forest. Grasping the fragile bundle to her chest, she doesn't need sight to know that the hungry things are watching.

She must protect the baby from them at all costs, there is too much at stake.

Ahead, jack-'o-lanterns encircle an impossibly desolate clearing with a primeval well at its centre.

Instinctively, the baby in her arms begins struggling, dusting the blanket with an amniotic crust.

The corpulent thing in the well yammers, wailing in anticipation of hot meat and tiny bones to grind in its teeth.

## Teeth

"Mummy, they hurt!" cried Zoe, pressing her fingers against her gums.

"Hush now, we all go through the change."

"But it's not fair!"

"Life isn't fair, sweetheart, look at Mr Glover from next door. He's old and frail, he can't even look after himself."

Zoe folded her lip over her extending teeth. "I know I'll be strong like Daddy soon, but, Mummy?"

"Yes, my little beastie?"

"Do I have to look at Mr Glover? He keeps twitching, I don't like it."

The old man wheezed, blood leaking from his neck.

"I've finished with him, now you start on the baby."

## Pumpkin Pasties

"Pumpkin pasties! Get your pumpkin pasties!"

Mike slipped a coin on the counter. "One, please."

"Here you go, nice and hot, made 'em myself."

He grabbed the pasty and wolfed it down.

His stomach twisted and gurgled.

"That didn't taste right," he moaned, between burps.

"Maybe you ate it too fast?" said the baker.

"Ugh, what was that? You said it was pumpkin."

"It is pumpkin, with a special Halloween ingredient."

Mike doubled over and spewed wriggling lumps of orange and green.

"You poisoned me!"

"No, I didn't. Do you know how hard it is to mince a live goblin?"

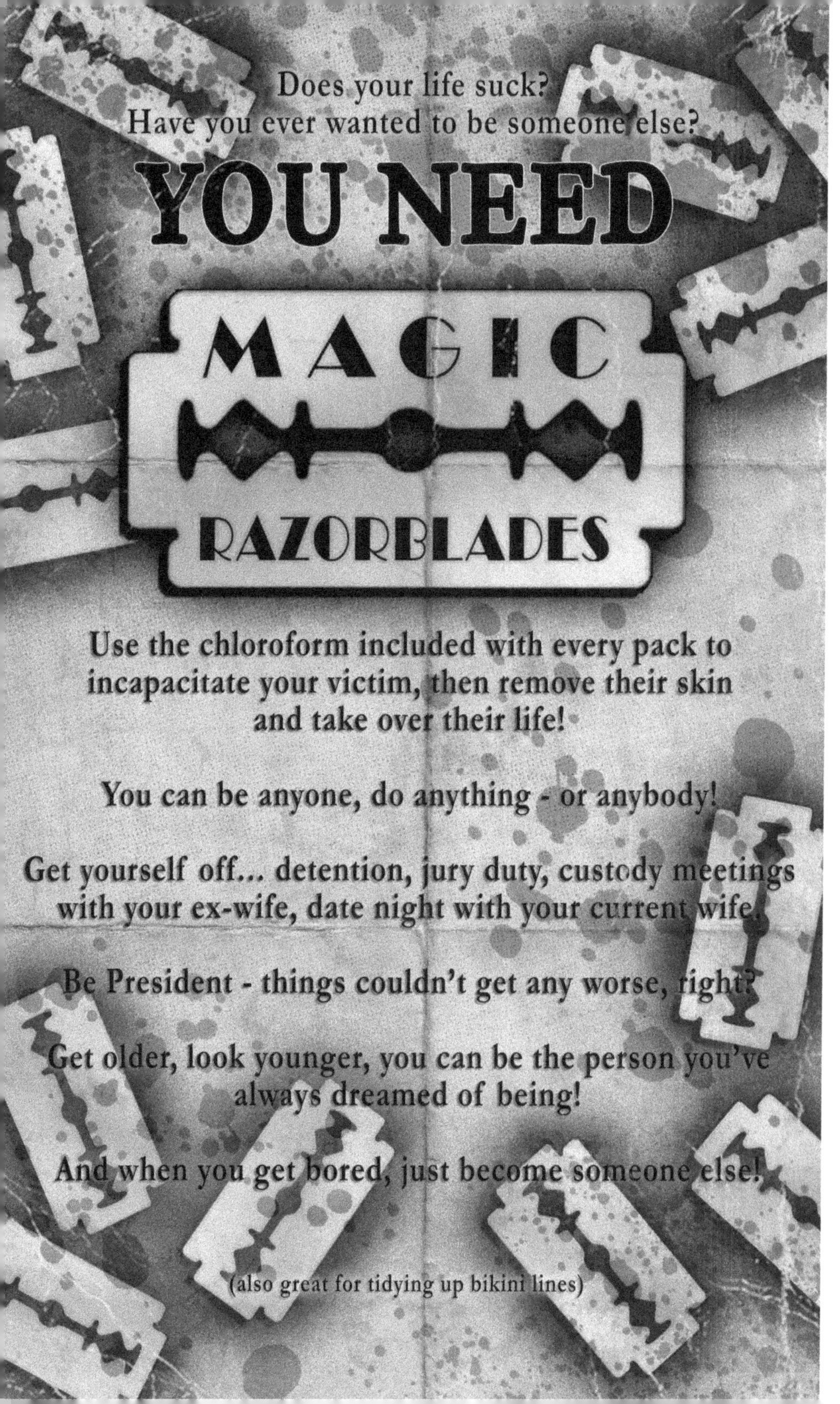
Does your life suck?
Have you ever wanted to be someone else?
YOU NEED
MAGIC
RAZORBLADES
Use the chloroform included with every pack to incapacitate your victim, then remove their skin and take over their life!
You can be anyone, do anything - or anybody!
Get yourself off... detention, jury duty, custody meetings with your ex-wife, date night with your current wife.
Be President - things couldn't get any worse, right?
Get older, look younger, you can be the person you've always dreamed of being!
And when you get bored, just become someone else!
(also great for tidying up bikini lines)

## The Home

Every year, the Star-lit Evening retirement home staff go *all out*.

From midnight, September 30th, pumpkin and bats adorn the corridors.

It makes some of the residents uncomfortable, but deteriorating minds tend to forget quickly.

The Halloween Hootenanny is always spectacular, they hire a DJ who picks the sort of vintage swing that the costumed wrinklies love.

But, no matter how much fun they have, or how young they feel, come lights out, the ravenous shambling thing will stalk the halls. Impossible fingers picking locks; as they do every night of the year.

Come morning, no-one ever remembers.

## Bespoke

Lisa lay on the table, tears streaming down her face.

She struggled; her numb body wouldn't respond.

The skin of her left arm was peeled back like a washing-up glove, if they sold them in putrefying-skin pink.

The surgeon began on her other arm whilst humming Monster Mash; his dark eyes looming from behind a vintage Frankenstein mask.

He sliced open her torso, shooting her a wink as he cut off her boobs and jiggled them.

Then, he carefully folded the skin and slipped it into a box.

Lisa squinted at a sign on the side: Lady Suits.

## Alice, Go to Sleep!

"Mummy, there's a monster under my bed."

"There's nothing there, Alice! It's bed time, now *get*."

"But Mummy, there really is. He was talking last night, I heard him. When it's late, he crawls through my window and hides in the dark."

"Really? Well, I guess I'd better check for this *monster* then."

"Hello, any monsters under here?" Mum drops to her knees and peers into the darkness, before vanishing.

"Mummy, where are you?"

"I'm under your bed, sweetheart."

"Mummy, your voice is all strange, is that really you?"

"Why don't you come under here with me and find out?"

## Premature Decoration

It's the same every year, around mid-September, my skin begins to crawl.

Used to wonder why my mother always put the decorations out early, wish I were still that naive. God, I miss her.

I hollow out the pumpkins automatically; carving out eyes, noses and mouths. It isn't important that they're pretty, only that they glare.

"It hates the staring." That's what mom used to say, before the night all the candles went out.

I'll never forget the thing's faceless face, or the sound it made as it scraped across the ceiling.

Now I only use battery-powered candles.

## The Scratching

Night after night, wherever I am, the thing scratches.

Unseen claws cleaving deep furrows into the naked pine of my closet door; the endless snarling filling the room with its rancid meat breath.

All I can do is lie in bed, my fists clenched beneath the useless blankets, molten tears streaming down my face.

For months, it's shadowed me.

At dusk, it's there; growling from within the nearest cupboard, beneath the aeroplane lavatory seat, or the boot of my car.

The few times I've been brave enough to peek, it stops dead.

Nothing but jagged shavings and flecks of saliva.

## Sex and Candy Apples

Katie danced around the punch bowl; a year's worth of planning had paid off. Groups of drunken teenagers huddled in dark corners, groping each other.

The stink of sex and candy apples permeated the room. It would be enough to attract them, then maybe they'd make her one of them.

*A vampire.*

Shadows crept along the lawn as they descended.

Unfortunately, Katie had miscalculated who she was going to attract.

Four hulking werewolves burst through the lounge window and ravaged the hormonal party-goers; tearing them limb-from-limb in a hurricane of fur and blood.

Katie shrugged, "Close enough."

## Money for Meat

One bare leg atop the glowing jack-'o-lantern, Mercy Stanford waited for her evening's only client.

His name didn't matter, but any man who was spending Halloween in her company was probably up to no good.

Normally she took the holiday off —her regulars usually had plans.

*

He was exactly what she'd expected: an obnoxious self-delusional prick with tiny hands, a bulging wallet, and a caricature comb-over.

She felt sorry for him, almost sorry enough to fuck him before she slit his throat and cut out his organs.

But that always lowered the price of the meat.

## Sinkhole

People say the sinkhole opened at midnight, September 30th in the Barker basement, but no-one really knows for sure.

The first anyone knew was when the building and the still-slumbering Barker family within, disappeared down its yawning gullet three days later.

The ravenous crevasse expanded quickly, devouring the supermarket and the Granger Church.

We thought things were at their worst when the taps ran dry, and there was nothing to eat but decaying jack-o'-lantern husks.

When the skulking monstrosities scrambled out of the darkness, ragged teeth bared, our grumbling bellies became the least of our problems.

## Shadow Man

The old man cowered in the corner of his workshop, broken toys scattered across the floor.

"Wait! Don't!"

"Not this time," a shadowy figure said, and snapped his spindly twig fingers.

"Why are you doing this?"

"Things are changing around here."

"We've had an agreement since the beginning of time, what's changed?"

"The world has. Yesterday's horrors are the joys of today."

His elongated fingers twisted into razor-like thorns. Hacking and slashing at Santa's chest, glitter and candy spewed from deep jagged wounds.

The old man slumped to the ground, dead.

"Now it's my turn," laughed the Shadow Man.

## 666

"You got the mark on you!"

The hunched old lady screamed at Trevor, as he crossed the road away from her.

It was the fourth time this week she'd screamed at him.

She'd turned up to his work, and followed him around the local supermarket, whooping and waving her hands at him.

Not only was it embarrassing, but it was starting to get scary.

That evening, when he drew the curtains, there she was, standing on his street, pointing at his crotch again, mouthing, "Devil".

How did she know he'd lost that bet and had 666 tattooed on his arse?

## The Devil's Holiday

"On the Devil's holiday, heathen grown-ups, who should know better, dress up their innocent little angels like Beelzebub's own horde and take them door-to-door - teaching them how to beg for handouts like filthy winos.

What is the world coming to?

Satanists are being glorified on the tube, movies are all premarital sex.

Drunks wander the streets, women dress like Satan's concubines, parading their bare flesh around, looking to lead God fearin' men astray."

The children on the porch looked up at old man Jethro,

"So, mister, are you going to give us any candy, or not?"

## The Pumpkin

The pumpkin had grown strong amongst hundreds of brothers, an autumn army of bulbous kin.

From his blackened eyes: a mournful stare, and his mouth: an evil grin.

*

Thousands before him had been picked to decorate revellers' porches. But this would be the year that all changed.

Their eyes blazing, the scowling pumpkin horde crawled into the town, drawn by the mocking laughter of masked children and the nauseating reek of boiled candy.

When they found them, they throttled them with their vines, tearing off their costumes and swallowing them whole.

Abandoned candy sacks and tattered clothes scattered the streets.

## That One Obligatory Zombie Story

Shutter doors rattled on the shopping centre, accompanied by the sound of hundreds of voices rasping, "Brains!"

Claire and her family hid between the festive "Gardening and Halloween costume" section on the second floor of Big Buy. It gave them the best chance of survival.

Gerry twisted a rake in his hands, as Claire applied corpse paint to herself and the kids.

Zombies were unusually popular this year.

Gerry's quick thinking saved the day, setting every escalator on *down*.

After nine days, the last of the zombies' rotting legs disintegrated, whilst trying to reach women's lingerie on the first floor.

## Cut Throat 'ard Cider

When the world feels bigger than it should, and your bills 'av gotta get paid
When life's all sorts of unkind, and all you wanna get - is laid
That's when Cut-Throat Cider ™helps the most
Life won't get better, but you will forget your woes.
We could tell you that it's 'cause our orchards are the best,
but that would be untrue.
Our apples are just like the rest, but if you 'eard our secret we'd 'ave to kill you.
So, indulge, relax, 'ave a glass or five.
Dead may not be great, but it's easier than alive.

## The Autumn Festival

The cider is free, and sweeter than the bare thighs on display at any Halloween party. It's crisper than autumn leaves, refreshing as an October breeze - goes down quicker than a $2 whore.

You don't drink it, but it sure as hell drinks you.

*

Two hours after the second keg was opened, the Autumn Festival was pandemonium. The grass, drenched in body fluids that weren't all blood. Hollowed-out severed heads, set aflame with lighter fluid, self-amputated genitals, remains of pets that couldn't slip their leashes.

Those still able to walk shambled back to town - to continue the party.

## Rein of Blood

"Stop lying!" Ben prodded his sister's arm.

"I am not!"

"Mum, Kelly said Santa doesn't exist!"

"That's right, Ben. After the seasonal wars of 2016, Santa's reign was overthrown. It's about the same time Cupid murdered the Easter Bunny."

"But I still got Christmas presents and Easter eggs!"

"Mother Nature picked up the slack until she had a nervous breakdown. Though, personally, I think there was a hostile takeover. They outsourced to China - far more efficient."

"Who's in charge now?"

Mum pointed out of the window at the torrential blood rain. "The Shadow Man, my son, he has the throne."

## I Told You So

Blood struck the windscreen, obscuring Margaret's view. "For Heaven's sake, is this ever going to stop?"

Her wipers smeared thick red across the glass.

Dave gripped her hand. "Hush, don't let him hear you saying things like that."

"It's not like it could get any worse. No sun for weeks. Everything is death and decay."

"Things can *always* get worse, we still have each other."

Margaret didn't see the first flaming boulder strike the road.

The second smashed through the roof, obliterating Dave's skull and forcing his spine out of his arse into the car's footwell.

"Fine, you were right."

# TERRIFY YOUR PARENTS!

# ASTOUND YOUR FRIENDS!

Make bullies piss their pants, then steal their organs, genitals, AND wallets!

Scare them to death (literally) with the all-new, one of a kind Fright Mask™ (excluding our 10,000 other customers)

Made from 100% genuine virgin flesh.
This bespoke, hand stitched item is guaranteed to change your life!
For the paltry price of one single soul - it doesn't even have to be yours!

Fill out the attached coupon with your name and address. Then, trick someone you hate into signing the dotted line and make this Halloween the best you've ever had!

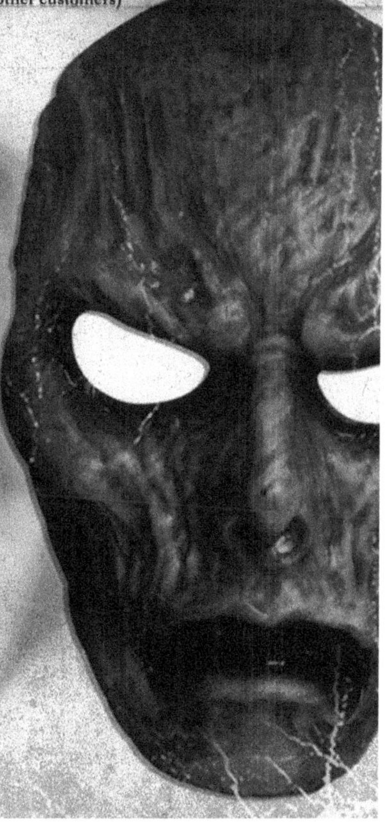

Please send my Fright Mask™ to:

Name (yours) _ _ _ _ _ _ _ _ _ _ _ _ _ _ _ _ _ _

Address (also yours) _ _ _ _ _ _ _ _ _ _ _ _ _ _

_ _ _ _ _ _ _ _ _ _ _ _ _ _ _ _ _ _ _ _ _ _ _ _

City _ _ _ _ _ _ State _ _ _ _ _ _ _ Zip _ _ _ _ _

**Signature**
of sucker paying _ _ _ _ _ _ _ _ _ _ _ _ _ _ _ _ _

## Poppet

Cody grips the poppet tight in pubescent hands, glaring at it with the burning fury of a thousand suns.

The doll has his father's self-righteous arsehole swagger, he thinks, which is a testament to Cody's sewing skills.

He knows his dad is asleep in the room down the hall; the image of him sleeping beside Alice is enough to make the boy's stomach turn.

Once this is over, he will get her all to himself. He will find out what she tastes like.

Cody twists the doll's head, and the shrill screams from down the hall fill the night.

## That Time of the Month

All month long she grooms like a fiend, exfoliating frantically, waxing legs, lips, and armpits before roaming tweezers pluck any stray hairs that dare to sprout in undesirable places. Her bathroom is heaped with organic face masks, body lotions, and shampoos, which boast every fragrance from freshly cut grass to bubblegum boom.

When the moon rises like an unshaded bulb, she drops the pretence. Relaxing into herself, she lets down her hair, allowing the waves of fur to sprout down the length of her spine like black weeds. Meticulously manicured French nails fall out, giving way to savage lupine claws.

## Candi

Mr Jenkins loved this time of year, big grins beneath caked face paint and Papier-mâché masks.

When his daughter lost her smile, crushed beneath the wheels of a speeding car, he'd snapped.

Candi's beaming pumpkin mask was all that remained of that fateful night.

*

Giggles filled the air. This year, their smiles would be the widest, and last forever.

His Halloween treats were crammed with an extra surprise. Candy that bites back, blades beneath their chocolatey flesh.

Placing them in unsuspecting buckets, he'd offer them the biggest smile of all.

"These are extra special, eat up, my little ones."

## Autumn Signal

Annually, the pumpkin lattes happen.

Adverts go out and the hordes of flesh comply, queueing for their fix.

Oblivious baristas fill paper cups with steamed milk and spiced foam.

Previously, it's been harmless, mostly.

But, this Halloween is special, it's the final sowing.

Through genuine smiles, patrons drink the minute spores, whilst within their bodies, saplings begin to down roots; they await the whisper from the Silent Vine.

Then, they will germinate, forcing thorny stems upward through organs, meat, and bone. Fronds break through skin and bear fruit.

This will be the greatest crop yet.

# Preening

Lucy had been prepping for the Monsters' Bash since 3PM.

She'd plucked her eyebrows into immaculate symmetricality, waxed her foof, and straightened her curls.

She didn't exactly slip into the little black dress, rather, she bullied her way into its constrictor embrace.

But, when she admired herself - it was totally worth it.

Her reflection grinned, much more than it should have.

Its foundation covered cheeks ripped almost to its ears.

Lunging, it dragged her backwards, leaving chunks of ragged meat dangling on jagged quicksilver shards.

When the Reflection arrived at the party, everyone said it looked phenomenal in that dress.

## The Old Ways are Best

Dean swung his shopping basket against his legs. "Why's everyone carving pumpkins? It's weird."

Stacy shrugged and continued down the aisle.

"I mean, is it a trend? There's pictures of people doing it, everywhere."

"I dunno, why don't you ask someone?"

"I *just* did!"

"Not me, stupid."

*

Stacy pointed to a row of knives, "Please, help me choose one."

"This one." He picked out a machete and smiled, "I love that we are traditionalists. By the way, what time did they say the toddler would be delivered? They're so much easier to carve creatively than newborns. Plus, *lots* more screaming."

## I Want Candy

Hayden scooped the last sticky piece from his Halloween bucket and stuffed it in his mouth. "I want *all* the candy."

The man in black crept forward, toes skimming the wrapper littered floor.

"I can give you what you want, but there will be a pri—"

"—Don't care, give me all the candy."

He grabbed the boy's lower jaw, stretching it wide, "Here you go."

He forced a bulging handful down the boy's throat.

Hayden retched and pulled away.

The man in black dragged him back, and yanked down his trousers. "Open wide, or I'll force it in another way."

## No More Candy

Hayden's mother wept as his extra-large coffin was lowered into the ground. The Halloween burial had been last-minute; after a year in a coma, his heart had failed.

The ropes were barely able to take the weight, as the coffin hit the bottom of the giant hole.

A clod of earth hit the box lid with a thud, followed by a single rose from his mother.

The man in black slunk from the shadows and floated towards the grave. He scattered a handful of candy on top of the dirt mound. "I'll be seeing you soon," he whispered.

## Friday the 31st

Joseph doesn't care about carving pumpkins or giving out Halloween candy.

At Casa Peters (population: one, not counting cockroaches) you will find no glow-in-the-dark skeletons, and a grand total of zero plastic bats.

His salary is barely sufficient to cover lights, water - or food.

Ignoring every knock at the door, Joe sits in the dark, stomach grumbling, his toes clenched beneath socks that have more holes in them than Trump's stories.

Joe thinks of his father, hopes the biopsy comes back negative.

He doesn't need to dress it up - life is scary enough.

And rent is due.

## The Old Gilligan House

Every town has those rumours about strange and dangerous neighbours.

A house with blacked-out windows, and black-hearted residents.

There was one at the end of Timmy's road.

"That's old Mr Gilligan's house, we don't go there," parents would whisper, leading their young swiftly past. "He eats children."

Timmy didn't believe his parents when Mr Gilligan welcomed him through the door.

He *still* didn't, as he was led to the kitchen for a "special treat".

Piles of flayed children's bodies, oozing blood, and dismembered limbs browning in the oven convinced him.

The kitchen door slammed shut, with him inside.

## I Don't Want Candy

Every Halloween, Hayden bolted the windows and doors, praying the man in black wouldn't return. But he always did.

This year was different; diabetes had ravaged his body.

He lay huddled in his hospital bed, surrounded by whirring machines, a long plastic tube forced down his throat.

Shadows crept beneath his door and smothered the room in a bitter darkness.

The man entered, wearing a toothless grin and dragging a large leather sack that squeaked on the linoleum.

"Happy Halloween, my boy. Open wide." — He squinted at the tube in Hayden's throat — "Well, I guess we'll need to get creative."

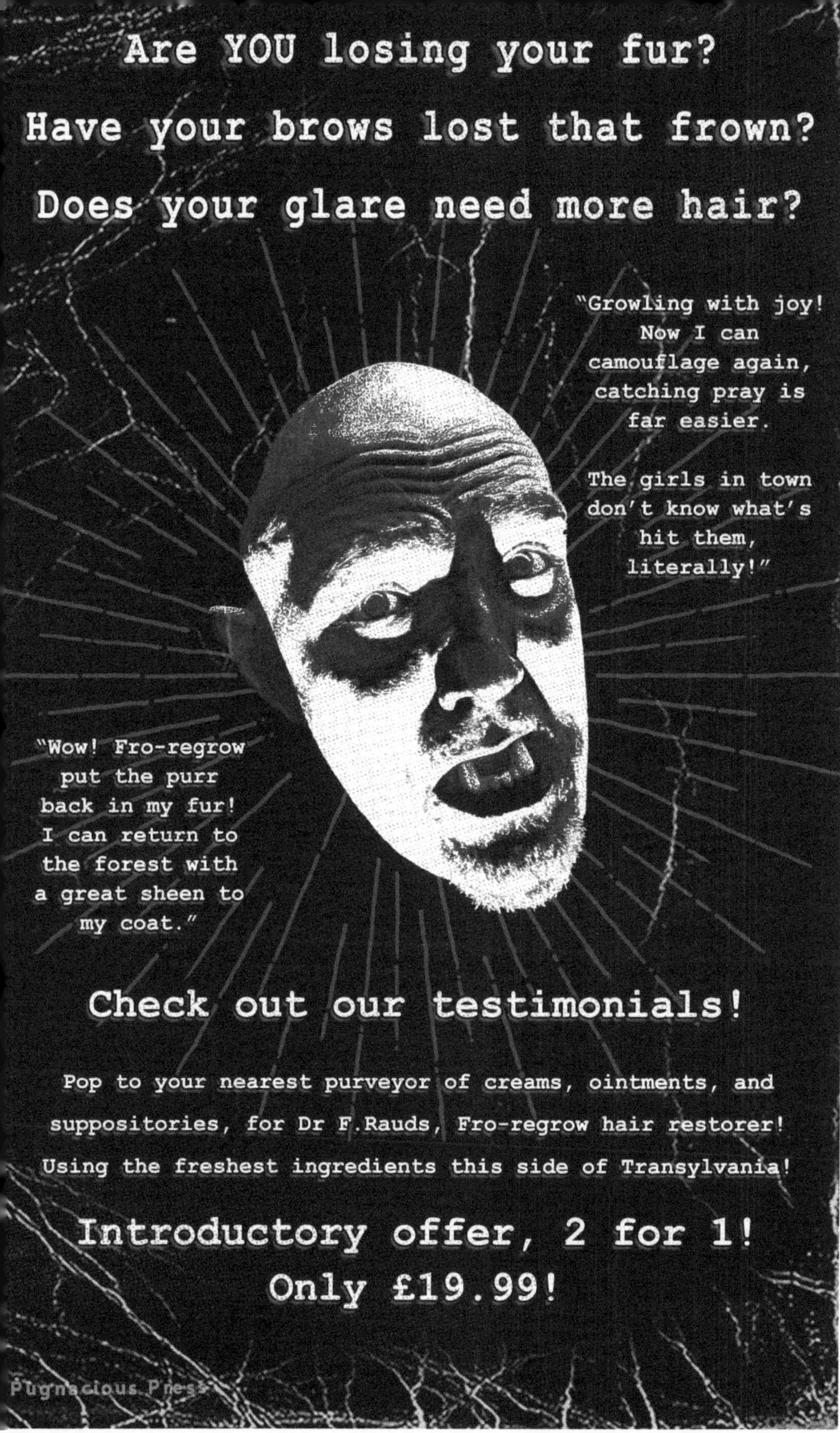
Are YOU losing your fur?
Have your brows lost that frown?
Does your glare need more hair?
"Growling with joy! Now I can camouflage again, catching pray is far easier.
The girls in town don't know what's hit them, literally!"
"Wow! Fro-regrow put the purr back in my fur! I can return to the forest with a great sheen to my coat."
Check out our testimonials!
Pop to your nearest purveyor of creams, ointments, and suppositories, for Dr F.Rauds, Fro-regrow hair restorer!
Using the freshest ingredients this side of Transylvania!
Introductory offer, 2 for 1!
Only £19.99!
Pugnacious Press

## The Man in Black

He always knows, the man in black.

On the lookout for deals, bargains of the flesh.

If you know his real name and call for him, he *will* come.

Fingers tapping at your window, spindly shadows growing on your floor.

He slips through the cracks of our world, caught in the gaps between whispered words. A hum in the silent dark.

"What is it you ask, my child?" he rasps, lips pulled tight over blackened, toothless gums.

Make sure once you've signed your contract, you're willing to pay the price.

He'll come for you when payment's due, ready to collect.

## But Nobody Cares

Every year, children go missing in Riverside, but that isn't news. It's not what people talk about at the office, cafes, or teetering against bars.

Sometimes the kids show up months later, what's left of them anyway; ragged pieces of flesh clogging storm drains, amid autumn leaves and bone brittle twigs.

Sometimes, their heads still have teeth, though more often not, tiny jaws crushed by rocks, noses and ears clipped off with what forensics are calling *pruning shears.*

But reporters aren't interested in any of that, they only ask me one thing:

"So, Detective, planning to fuck any more sheep?"

## Free Porn

"Jackie boy, goddamn it —get over here – you're missing the good stuff!"

Jack flew through the house to where Alistair was hanging out by the TV.

"Oh my god, that's magnificent!"

They watched the semi-naked trio on the couch going at it like mad things. A buxom brunette in cat ears sat on Papa Smurf's face, whilst a blonde in only a hooded robe and witch nose bounced on his cock.

Alistair and Jackie went for a high five, but, as always, their ghostly hands passed through each other.

"I swear, being dead at Halloween sure has some benefits."

## Bring the Kettle

"Just hot water, please," the old man said, taking a seat in the café.

The barista brought it to the table.

He ushered the girl back to the kitchen. "No, it needs to be hotter."

She returned momentarily, water bubbling in her hands.

He grabbed it and poured the boiling liquid down his throat.

"More," he rasped.

The girl returned again and again.

"I need more," he whispered, through blistered lips.

"Sir, this isn't safe."

"I have to stop it."

"Stop what?"

He pointed to his bleeding mouth, "I have to kill it."

Inside his throat, a bulbous eye blinked.

## The Great Thing About Lines

Chris is happy to wait in queues, it's nice knowing there's someone standing behind him. It's then that he can relax, he can ignore the sensation of frigid fingers brushing the back of his neck, he can pretend that the person standing behind him in the line is just friendly.

*Super friendly.*

But whilst he knows better, nevertheless, sometimes it's nice to pretend.

When he leaves the store and traverses the autumn street, he isn't alone.

He spends each night, spine pressed into the corner; the thing on his back dragging its calloused fingers down the nape of his neck.

## Urban Legends

"Bloody letters covered the wall, and they read, 'AREN'T YOU GLAD YOU DIDN'T TURN ON THE LIGHTS?'"

Scoutmaster Ned's tale was met with nothing but the sound of crickets.

The blank-faced kids around the campfire stared absently into the flames.

"That wasn't scary," came a small voice from the back. A chorus of agreement rose.

"Alright then, hard stuff, you tell me a scary story."

The eight-year-old produced a cellphone, and following a few deft taps, handed it to Ned.

"This one's called Two Girls One Cup," he said.

Scoutmaster Ned would never sleep soundly again.

## The Bride

Beware the bride who was buried alive. If you've done her wrong, she'll find you.

That flash of white in the corner of your eye, that's her. Her dirt-encrusted mouth will whisper your name.

She's looking for a love to take back to the grave.

Elongated arms trailing at the sides of her torn wedding dress. On All Hallows Eve your front door won't stop her, neither will the numerous locks.

Her spindly fingers of shadow tear eyes from sockets, and tongues from screaming mouths.

Remember: don't look back, for if you catch her gaze, it's already too late.

## Click, Hiss, Click, Hiss

Mark turns the TV on, and off, on, off, and on again.

The static whispers, before the "Ultra realistic" image fills the 85-inch pixel perfect monitor.
Of all the things in the world - it's him mirrored on screen, but not as he knows himself.

Yes, he's sitting on the 12-grand leather couch - but his face is twisted beyond recognition. Severed cheeks flap loose from his yellowing skull, dripping gore onto his white chinos.

There's a shadow, too, hovering over his left shoulder.

But it's not behind him, he's looked - it's only on the TV.

It moves closer every time he turns it off.

## You Know You Want To

"Go on, Nancy, give it a rub."

Throbbing red lights hid her frown.

"No, I'm not doing that."

"Please, just touch it."

"No!"

"Not even the top? Just give the top a rub."

"I'm not that kinda girl - I know the others might have been, but I'm not."

"Spoil sport. I don't care 'bout the other girls, you're here with me."

She sighed and shook her head.

Billy slipped the black pulsating lamp back onto the antique shop shelf, between the Necronomicon and a puzzle box. "Fine."

"Look, I'm not brave enough to risk my soul on three stupid wishes."

## Thirst

Sometimes, I wonder when it will stop, the thirst.

My Friday nights used to be drunk, down at the pub. The beer would flow, then the shots… then the vomit.

Sometimes, I'd get lucky. More often than not, I wouldn't.

The night *she* found me, I was lying in the gutter in my Dracula costume, covered in more than *one* of my bodily fluids.

She held me and gifted me the eternal kiss.

*

My tastes have changed since then; the thirst hasn't.

I still skulk around the pub on a Friday, looking for something delicious to drink.

Perhaps you're next.

## The Trio

"First of the night, always special," —whispered the pale boy in the pinstriped suit. He corrected the alignment of his greased blond hair with a clawed hand, and flashed a piranha-toothed grin at his two companions.

The tallest wore a black robe, red eyes flickering beneath a cowl.

The shortest, merely a beach ball with feet, under the filthiest sheet imaginable.

The looming house glowed orange, jack-o-lanterns covering its face like molten pimples.

A middle-aged man in full dentist garb opened the door. Smiling, he fanned out a rainbow coloured assortment of toothbrushes.

He'd never walk again.

## Sheet Ghost

The diminutive sheet ghost stood on the street corner at the edge of Sleeping Oaks cemetery.

"Hey, you fat shit!" Billy Jones had never been one for subtlety, especially in front of his numerous cronies.

"Leave me alone, or you will regret it."

The high-pitched voice didn't match the beach ball girth beneath the ragged filthy sheet.

Billy stuck an arm under the sheet, bent on twisting the child's nose, but there *was* no nose. Instead, his hand slipped into a frigid, wet maw. Jaws clamped down around his forearm, Billy's world disintegrated into the sound of crunching bones.

## Three Reasons Why

Suit's candy haul had been sub-par, although there were certainly benefits to being short changed - like razor-blading any unwanted apples and then sneaking them back into the offending fuck's goodie bowl. Failing that, he could always collect some more ears.

Grinning, he patted his bulging pocket, and the red splotch on the pinstriped fabric expanded.

Testing the weight of his candy sack, he decided it was time to change tactics.

Approaching the rabble of costumed children on the corner, Suit slid out his Stanley knife, and, in his most seductive voice, explained why they should fill his fucking bag.

## The Thing on the Porch

Charlotte furrowed her emerald-painted forehead, and looked down on the black-robed figure that stood on her doormat.

"Candy." It spat.

Contemplating the unnerving glowing red eyes, she imagined parents arriving with police to adjust her "attitude", with words like "litigation" and "register."

She sighed, and selected a measured response to the insolent little shit.

"What's the magic word?"

Undeterred, the grim reaper glared up, its red eyes flickering beneath the hood. It held out a gaping pillowcase.

"Give me fucking candy, or I'll cut you open and hang your guts from that tree."

She didn't, so it did.

## Whisper Lake

Peter grabbed Stefan and headed for the front door — "Dad, we're going to the lake!"

They set off through the town and dumped their bikes at the edge of the woods, beside Whisper Lake.

They dove in, racing each other to the centre.

Peter grabbed Stephan's foot, twisting and squeezing. Stephan kicked out to loosen Peter's grip.

He peered beneath the surface.

*No Peter.*

A long white tentacle coiled up his ankle and yanked his leg - tearing it free from the socket. Stephan screamed and struggled against the creature's grasp.

It was too late.

He was wrenched into the depths.

## The Caustic Tale of Emily Brown

Emily placed her four aces on the table. "I win, now you do what I want. On your knees."

Alex obeyed.

She pulled her skirt up, revealing crotchless panties, and locked her legs around his neck.

She clenched her thighs, "Your turn to weep."

His tongue, now buried deep inside her, began to bubble and dissolve.

Emily giggled, "Oh Alex, that tickles."

His lips peeled away from his teeth, melting, and dribbling down his chin.

She squeezed again, forcing his entire head inside her. It fizzled and popped off his twitching body.

"I'll save the rest for later," she grinned.

## The Inflatable Pumpkin Vampire

Being thirty had its benefits: casual sex, disposable income, and making coffee nude – but, if you lost a bet, you paid up.

Sally waddled hysterically at top speed for three blocks, her outfit squeaking every single goddamn mother fucking step of the way.

Sweat streamed into her eyes as she fumbled with the lock, and then got stuck in the door jamb like Winnie the Pooh.

As the vampire closed in on her, fangs bared, Sally cursed the giant inflatable pumpkin costume that Jenny had made her wear.

*If I come back as a blood-sucker, you're dead, Jen, I fucking swear.*

## Paul Likes to Decorate

He carved a hole in the top of its head, mutilating tough flesh. Vicious hands clawed at its insides, tearing out the rancid guts, soon to be baked in a pie.

Two triangular holes for eyes, and a little one for the nose. An evil grin of jagged teeth, and it would be complete.

*

"Darling, I'm finished —do you want to light him?"

"What? Paul, what did you do?"

He shrugged. "Suit yourself."

He lit a stumpy candle and slipped it inside, admiring his work. Every year, around Halloween, Paul went a bit funny, and the neighbour's cats began vanishing.

## Mice in the Attic

Theresa shuffled under her duvet and pointed to the ceiling, "Something's up there."

"It's just mice," said Emma.

"It sounds like footsteps."

"Wanna go look?"

"N-no thanks."

"Fine, go to bed!"

*

"Theresa…" A voice fractured the serenity.

"Em, did you…"

Her sister was asleep.

"Theresa, come here…" It came from a vent above her bed.

She clambered up and peered inside: nothing.

The front popped loose and bounced onto her duvet.

Bony arms twisted out of the vent and snatched her from the bed.

She screamed as it yanked her through the tiny metal hole, back into its realm.

ARE YOUR ENCHANTMENTS UN-ENCHANTING?
PLAGUES NOT SO PLAGUING?
CURSES NOT SO CURSIVE?
C'MON DOWN TO WILBUR WAILS
CAULDRON SALE!
BIG, SMALL, IRON, PEWTER, COPPER,
WE'VE GOT THEM ALL!
SCARE YOUR FRIENDS, CURSE YOUR ENEMIES,
AND DO IT WITH STYLE.
ARE THOSE TWO PESKY CHILDREN STILL MUNCHING ON
YOUR CANDY HOUSE?
BUY ONE CAULDRON, AND GET ONE FREE.
COOK BOTH KIDS AT THE SAME TIME,
NO MATTER HOW MUCH YOU FATTEN THEM UP!
WILBUR WAILS
CAULDRON
SALE!
100%
GLUTEN
FREE!
YOU NEED AN UPGRADE!
OUR LATEST SCALD-O-MATIC, WITH NEW SELF-STIRRING MOTOR.
Behind Salty Sals' bar on Doom N' Gloom Lane.

## The Inflatable Pumpkin Vampire Bounces Back!

"You hear squeaking?"

Michael gulped his beer and stared at Kevin.

"You're annoying when you're drunk."

"It sounds like a rubber duck orgy."

"Just bats. Drink up, girls are waiting."

Kev pointed to the far side of the football pitch — "Tell me you see that."

Waddling on green stockinged legs, a giant pumpkin emerged from the night. It headed towards them at what would be considered top speed for a marshmallow.

Jaws snapping ferociously, the vampire within the inflatable pumpkin leapt at the boys.

The costume kept her far enough away that they needn't have worried… She kept bouncing off.

## The Room

My room is exactly the same as when I went to bed - but totally not.

The paint feels a fraction of a shade off from the eggshell white I'd meticulously selected.

*What's that smell? The bedsheets?*

The sunshine blotting the curtains is off.

*Too bright? Not bright enough?*

My mouth is dry, and my bladder full - I wait as long as I can before I get up.

*Was the bed always this high?*

I reach for the door handle, but there isn't one.

Instead, a near-perfect copy of my door is painted onto the wall - that definitely isn't eggshell.

## Samhain in the Woods

"Let's go camping at Ashbourne woods for Halloween," Mandy said. "We'll dress up, sit around the campfire, get smashed - it'll be great!"

*

3AM, drunk as fowls and laughing like psychopaths, we all collapsed in the tent.

When the shrieking began outside, we started awake.

A gritty cacophony of cancerous screaming and clanging rusted gates.

The second Clara undid the zip, the wailing stopped - but *she* saw what had been making it.

Now silent, the blind, faceless things encircled the tent, their elongated bodies quivering.

Clara sealed the flap, her stomach writhing eels, and again, the guttural chorus filled the night.

## Witches

"I don't want to be a pumpkin this year, I want to be a witch," Nicole whined.

"Don't be silly, we can't dress that way in our house."

"But mum—"

"—No! I don't care how your friends are dressed."

Jane peered out of the window at the Halloween bonfire, flames coursing up to the sky. A bound girl struggled as she was led towards the crackling pyre, her screams punctuating the crisp autumn air.

"We must be careful and stay hidden. At least until the town stops suspecting witchcraft, or the plague takes hold, then we can be ourselves again.

## Got Wood?

Jim was dragged into court; hands cuffed and head hanging.

"You, sir, are charged with negligence," said the judge. "Twelve women have died and several are injured because of your poor broom craftsmanship."

"How was I supposed to know they'd do that? Everything was up to code."

"They're witches, what did you expect them to do with a broomstick?"

"Yes, I know, *fly*. But it says in the maintenance clause we're not responsible for misuse."

"This wasn't a case of misuse."

"How could I know they'd grip them better without their knickers on? I couldn't have accounted for excess splinters!"

## Regrettable Ink

Napalm tears burned down Parker's cheeks, his eyes piss holes in the snow.

His thoughts clawed hatefully at the images playing on a loop in his skull: Lizzie's bare breasts bouncing as she ground her softest parts against a man who certainly wasn't him.

Parker tore off his ragged shirt and peeled the cling film wrap from his chest, revealing the anatomical heart now etched into his skin in red and black ink.

Around it, Lizzie's name exquisitely executed in cursive.

There was only one thing for it.

Gripping the straight razor, Parker began to cut her out of his life.

## But, Little did he Know

"Star light, star bright. The first star I see tonight; I wish I may, I wish I might, get the wish I wish tonight."

Leo stared up at the sky and crossed his fingers, unaware his wish was coming true as his rather obnoxious wife balanced her charging phone on the side of their ludicrously expensive bathtub, and slipped into the bubbling water.

BZZZT.

Lights flickered in the lounge, before smothering him in darkness; accompanied by the overwhelming stench of cremated bacon.

Thank goodness for insurance policies, stupidity, and Jacuzzi whirl-tubs.

At least he could pay the bills now.

## Shocker

A naked Matt lay on the floor of his glass cell. The stench of acrid sulphur and rot made him retch. Vomit struck the floor, shooting sparks against the walls.

Electricity crackled across the ceiling in streaks of blue.

Creatures writhing on tentacles stalked the hallway outside.

He shivered, unsure of how he'd got there.

The last thing he remembered was crashing onto his beanbag, loading up his laptop, and starting his story edits.

A creature stroked its tentacles against the wall, the glass popped and melted, leaving a gaping, molten hole.

"Time. To. Stand. Trial," the grotesque creature hissed.

## "In my House" by Samantha Watson, Age 4

Four people live in my house, mommy is the definitely the most prettiest. Daddy calls her sugar and he kisses her on the lips. Mommy likes it a lot, but I think it's icky.

I love when daddy takes me for ice-cream, he puts me on his shoulders and says I'm his favouritist.

He's always smiling. Except when Josh makes funny noises from the basement.

Mommy doesn't like it, she says Joshua is naughty.

Josh only ever shushes after daddy takes the plank downstairs and asks him nicely.

I'm glad I don't have to share mommy and daddy anymore.

## Knock All You Like

Nick pointed at his neighbour's window, "Gotta love these realistic projector decorations."

A ghostly, pale green figure flew towards the window in a loop, waving a severed head at passers-by.

His son rooted around his bag of candy, "I guess, it's not very scary."

"What about Mr Peterson's across the street?"

The silhouette of a hanged man twitched, swaying in the window.

"It's a bit better, I guess."

Despite the feverish knocking of candy-hunting children, his door wasn't answered that night, or any night thereafter.

When Peterson's rotting decorations were still up in December, people started getting concerned.

## The All Hallows Monster Movie Marathon

The 'All Hallows Monster Movie Marathon' drive-in screen glowed like an impossible moon against the overcast night.

But, from the backseat of her dad's Camaro, Roxy didn't care. Eight minutes earlier, Brian had slipped his hand up her shirt. She knew that the warmth of his palm was something she'd never ever forget.

Two cars away, Evelyn Stefan's throat was being ripped out by a creature wearing a man's face. A beast hungry for more than illicit groping and overpriced popcorn.

It was two days before the Drive-in staff realised that her body wasn't a discarded Halloween prop.

## Glory Hole

Alex knelt, waiting eagerly beside the glory hole. He'd done this a couple times before; always fun, and he loved a surprise.

Footsteps.

His heart raced; someone was coming to join him. His glory-friend slipped into the next cubicle.

The sound of jeans unzipping made him throb. Lips locked to the hole, he waited.

It was warm, wet, and wriggling.

*Wait, that isn't right. Why is it wriggling?*

He gagged.

It pushed further into his mouth and slid down his throat, the force slamming him against the cubicle wall.

A tentacle pulsated inside his stomach and deposited its eggs.

## Anything for Love

Betty has always been a "difficult" woman, but Seymour loves her despite this.

Mostly he loves her the firmness of her ass, her legs, her chest. But, he loves her most when her mouth is too full to talk.

So, when she said she wanted THE ring, there was no question in his mind - but, after looking at the extortionate price-tag, he'd have get a little creative.

*

He decided that Halloween was the best time to go ring shopping. With all the screaming and fake blood, it would be easy pickings for a man with chloroform and pruning shears.

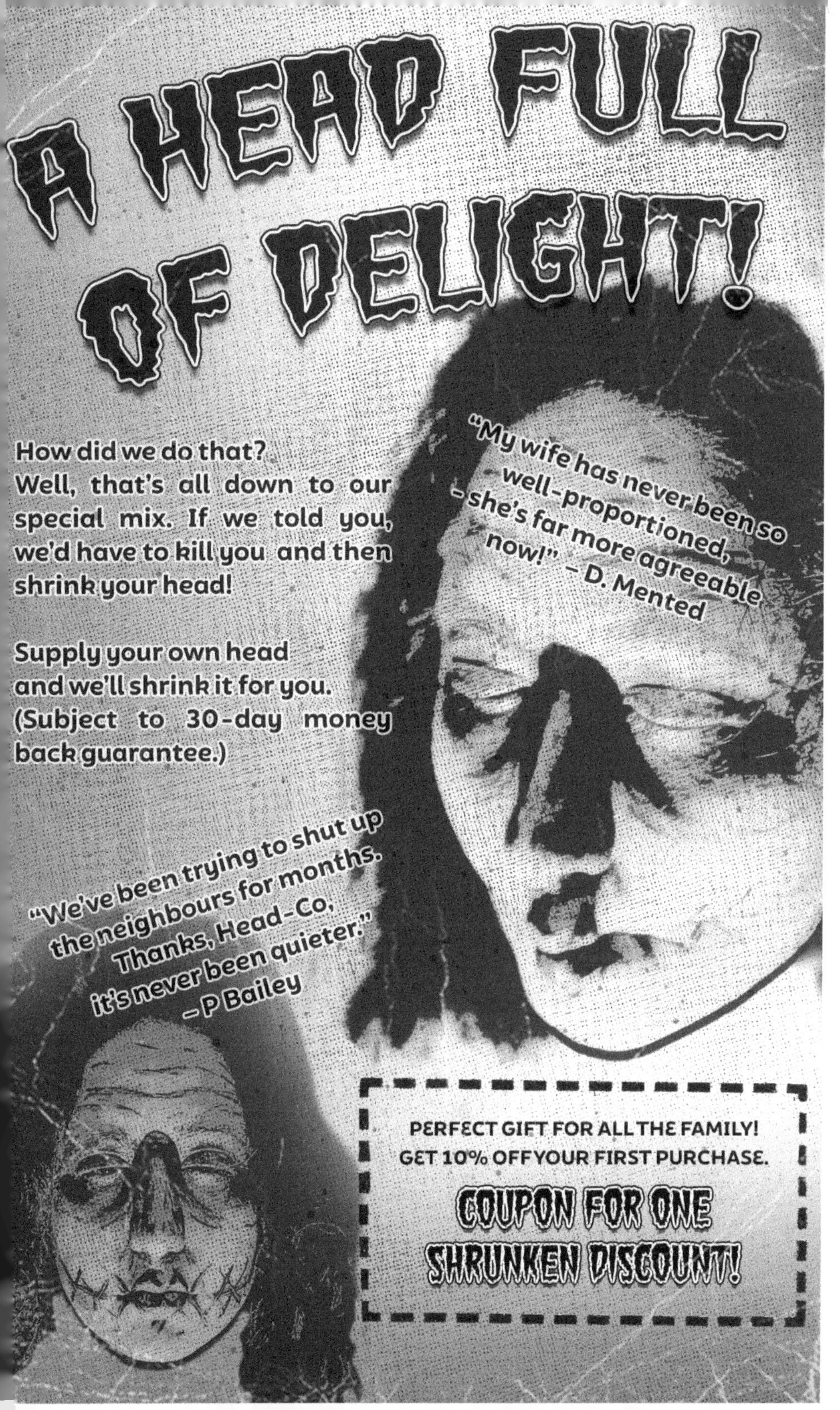
A HEAD FULL OF DELIGHT!
How did we do that?
Well, that's all down to our special mix. If we told you, we'd have to kill you and then shrink your head!
Supply your own head and we'll shrink it for you. (Subject to 30-day money back guarantee.)
"My wife has never been so well-proportioned, - she's far more agreeable now!" – D. Mented
"We've been trying to shut up the neighbours for months. Thanks, Head-Co, it's never been quieter." – P Bailey
PERFECT GIFT FOR ALL THE FAMILY!
GET 10% OFF YOUR FIRST PURCHASE.
COUPON FOR ONE SHRUNKEN DISCOUNT!

## Home is Where the Heart Is

Do you know why they brick up the windows on houses? You don't? That's good, because I'll tell you.

Sometimes you might hear people say, "Daylight Robbery" - but that's a lie.

Inside that forgotten, bricked-up room, beats the heart of the home.

Most houses are dead now.

Knocking down walls and building extensions, eventually something's gotta give.

Others thrive, feeding on their owner's energy, or some other unlucky victim.

The dulcet throb behind those walls isn't the central heating.

Come Halloween, no mischief will befall the doorstep of living houses, for they are watching and waiting for more delicious visitors.

## Blood-Spatter Prints™

Damien pawed through piles of t-shirts on the stall. “So, you’re the guy who makes those Blood-Spatter shirts?”

“Yup.” said Harry.

“I could make better ones.”

“Really?”

“Yeah, doesn’t look hard. Just mess around with Photoshop, everyone’s doing it.”

“I have a very special method. If you hang on after closing, I’ll show you how it’s done.”

*

He threw a t-shirt to Damien. “Put this on.”

Damien shrugged, but did as instructed, “I don’t get it.”

Harry slipped a knife from his back pocket, “Oh, you will,” and stabbed him.

“Well, there’s my latest design sorted.”

## Waiting for Sleep

Nelson peered out from under the bed, watching and waiting.

*BANG*! The door flew open, accompanied by shrieks of joy. Tiny feet clambered onto the soft bedding; jumping up and down, driving dagger-like broken springs closer to his face.

*

Worn out, the children collapsed, snuffled sleeping breaths filling the air.

His stomach twisted. He couldn't hide here all night, he had work to do.

He'd been doing this for years, and yet, the first scare session at a new house always made him nervous.

Nelson adjusted his horns and skittered out from beneath the bed.

*Here we go again.*

# It Waits

It lurks on the top shelf when the lights go out. Nestled in the shadows between an ageing porcelain doll and a ragged teddy, it watches. Unblinking eyes survey the room, as they have done nightly since the soulless thing arrived.

It regards the small body dozing below as each new breath shifts the sailboat-dappled duvet.

It is hungry, it's *always* hungry.

The creature's once immaculate white fur is now matted with a crust of sticky decaying sweets. It bides its time, the waiting ever as much a part of the hunt as the feeding.

Furby is ever patient.

## Look, Mommy!

Last Halloween, Tyler found a severed hand on the pavement just outside his house.

When he showed it to his mom, she squinted at her phone and said "That's nice, sweetie, why don't you go play in your room?"

Gingerly, Tyler put the hand in his recently-vacated hamster cage.

He gave it fresh sawdust, and grapes, just in case it was hungry - it wasn't.

It was a full week before he came to the conclusion that it was never going to move from the spot in the corner where he put it.

Also, it stank worse than dad's feet.

## Autumn Loving

Hand-in-hand, we ran down the moonlit hillside, naked as the day we were born. Limbs fuelled by Halloween candy and pilfered cider, we bounded over tombstones, cheeks aching from the ceaseless laughter, lips buzzing electricity from hours spent kissing behind the antiquated Riverside church.

We reached the edge of the forest, and within seconds Caleb had torn free of his ruddy human skin, to reveal an ashen pelt. I delighted in the sensation as the false flesh fell away and my features returned to their natural shape.

Caleb led the hunt, and I followed blissfully on all fours.

## Silence

Jerry liked the silence.
His neighbours, despite repeat requests refused to quieten down, blared shit music at all hours.

No matter how often he complained, the police were uninterested in his plight.

His neighbours didn't hear him enter through the shutter door that night.

Nor his footsteps on the wooden floor, creaks hidden beneath thumping drum and bass.

Blood trickled from his head and stained his crisp white shirt.

The rusty screwdriver he had thrust into his ears brought the sweet release of silence.

It would soon do the same for his neighbours, and bring the sweet release of death.

## Bargain Bin

Tara rummaged around the cardboard bargain bin.

*C'mon, nope, nope, maybe. Hmm …nope.*

She shoved a couple of DVDs under her arm and wandered the comic book store.

Shopping alone was a regular pastime, and the best way to find a good deal.

*Oh, what's this?*

Halloween treats and Spooky Surprises, HALF PRICE!

She dove into the bin up to her elbows, it was warm and sticky inside.

The deeper she dug, the hotter it got.

Something rough and wet stroked her hand before coiling her wrist like a hungry snake. It yanked her into the display stand, swallowing her whole.

## Brush All You Like

Dave wakes up every morning with blood on his pillow. It crusts his chin in an obscene scarlet beard.

His mouth filled with the flavour of old pennies, he does what he does every morning, and counts his remaining teeth.

*Not good.*

The number is already in single digits.

Dave tongues the fresh gap as he contemplates going out with a hammer and collecting teeth, but quickly realises that he doesn't have the malice in his spirit for such an endeavour.

After checking his savings account, he decides to hire a prostitute.

He hopes the fairies will take hers instead.

## Beast in the Bedroom

Her bed creaked. Or was it the wind outside? Faye didn't like noises that invaded her home at night. This was different. A scratching, grinding sound, like nails on a chalk board. She screwed her eyes shut, and wished them away.

Thud. The window flew open. Cold night air whipped the covers from her naked body, followed by a gigantic hairy fist that tore her from the bed. She clawed at the mattress, but it yanked her free and out of the window. Face-to-face with a gigantic beast, it stole her away into the night's inky blackness.

## Ghost

I don't know if you've had a ghost in your bedroom, but I have.

At night the spectral beast clambers in my window, forcing his horns against the frame until it pops open.

I've tried to seal him out, but he always finds a way.

Once inside, he torments me, bumping and banging. His monstrous bleating calls wake my family, but no one will help me.

Whipping away my bedsheets, he grinds and chews the fabric (I'm sick of replacing them).

Then, he escapes into the darkness.

I realise I may have made a spelling error at the start of this story.

## Clowning Around

Hundreds of kids joined the annual Halloween gathering on the White House lawn.

*HONK.* A clown squeezed his flower, spraying the audience. Children shrieked, waving their hands in the red misted air, droplets melting though their face paint.

He bowed, and cartwheeled out of the big top, as a troupe of dancing acrobats entered.

Slipping into a small camouflaged tent, away from the crowd, the clown yanked his sleeve, then tapped his ear piece. "Job's done Sir, 24 hours until we see results."

"Good work, Eads, we can't have any more of these youngsters growing up with opinions and ideas."

## When the Nightmares Come

The nightmares are sentient molasses slopping around my ankles.

But that's nothing new, not really.

They wait until I'm at ease, eyes shut, my mind flickering between here and that place on the far side, but tonight feels anything but normal.

I do what I can to resist, but they know - it's only a matter of time before exhaustion drags me down into the place where I can't escape.

Their breath is suffocating smoke, their eyes septic emeralds glowing in the dark.

They clasp arctic bramble fingers around my shoulders, wrists, and ankles.

Forcing me down, they fulfil their desires.

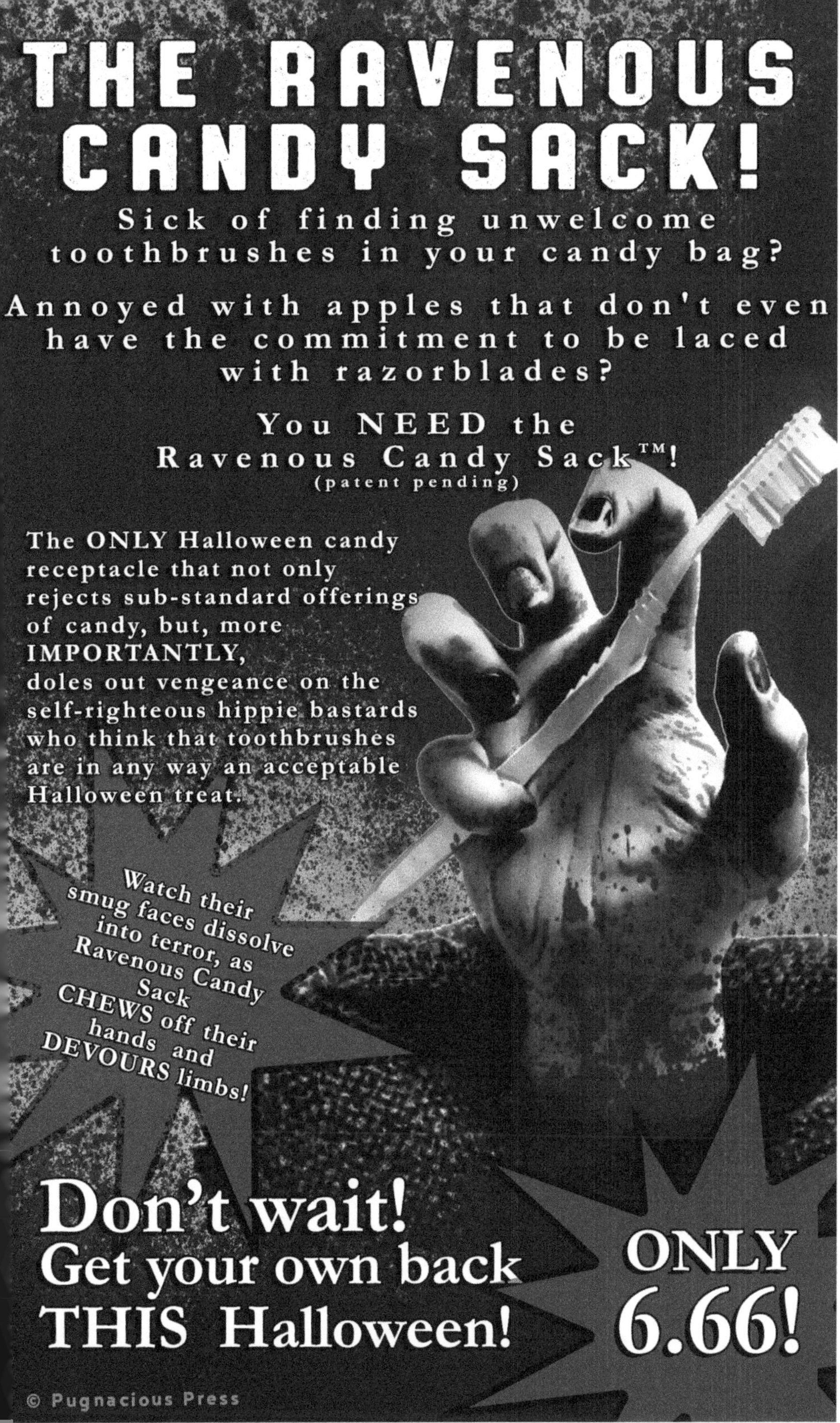
THE RAVENOUS CANDY SACK!
Sick of finding unwelcome toothbrushes in your candy bag?
Annoyed with apples that don't even have the commitment to be laced with razorblades?
You NEED the Ravenous Candy Sack™!
(patent pending)
The ONLY Halloween candy receptacle that not only rejects sub-standard offerings of candy, but, more IMPORTANTLY, doles out vengeance on the self-righteous hippie bastards who think that toothbrushes are in any way an acceptable Halloween treat.
Watch their smug faces dissolve into terror, as Ravenous Candy Sack CHEWS off their hands and DEVOURS limbs!
Don't wait! Get your own back THIS Halloween!
ONLY 6.66!
© Pugnacious Press

## Pure Evil

I am a demon of the night,
I've a sheen of ebony as I take flight.
Throughout history, I've been feared,
I am vampirically revered.
My body's furry, black as coal,
and I am here to take your soul.
Late at night you'll hear my call,
As I brush past your hair, your skin will crawl.
When the moon has risen in the sky,
I'll flap about and eat some flies.
I'm made of fur, teeth, and wings, and lots of other horrible things.
I don't cope well with fireworks or cats.
I am a Bat.

## The Lump

It started as an innocuous pimple below Lilian's earlobe, but, within a week, it had grown. If *grown* was even the right word.

By Tuesday, she'd have given her left ovary for it to still be boil-sized.

Her neck ached with the weight of the lump, which hung like a pendulous tit from her aching shoulder.

The weight cut off her circulation, leaving Lil's right arm with perpetual pins and needles.

*

Pain woke her on October 31st; shrieking cut through her senses like a knife.

Puckered skin on the boil split, as the screeching creature chewed its way out.

## The Old One

I curled my toes, digging deeper into the wet sand.

Ocean spray misted the foul air as bubbles rose from the depths.

One bulbous tentacle whipped foam from the rough grey sea. It tore clouds from the sky and blotted out the sun.

From one tentacle to multiple pulsating white legs, it drew itself into our world.

I was too scared to run, too in awe of this magnificent beast, this god.

I thumbed through the book, dark pages dampened by the lashing waves.

"Come forth to me, my destiny."

The creature shrieked and called down my glorious hell on earth.

## Post-its

The post-it is luminous pink.

*Ecstasy, this way*, it reads, a line of X's beneath. A waft of familiar citrus perfume, as I pluck it from the door, and step inside. There's another on the picture frame.

*This way.*

An arrow directs me towards the kitchen. A third on the fridge door.

*X*

I open it.

A severed arm dangles from the top shelf. Thumb and forefinger missing.

My pulse begins to churn.

A Woman's head in a bowl. Lip trembling, I stare into the back.

There, is the most perfect tuna sandwich ever constructed.

I love that woman.

## Black Magic Beans

Xander was thrilled with his candy haul.

Still in his skeleton onesie, he tipped the bag onto his bedroom floor. Assorted candies, and a tiny packet of black "Magic beans."

He asked his sister if she'd help plant them, but Susie cut him off.

"Don't be stupid, they're novelty jelly beans!" — She swallowed a fistful to reiterate her point, but Xander was unconvinced.

At 3AM, after an apparent earthquake had rocked the house, they discovered Susie.

Her ribcage puckered outwards, splintered bones encircling the base of a tremendous black stalk that pierced the ceiling and climbed into the sky.

## Tall Tail

"You're not my mum!" Nigel grimaced, as the woman slipped a plate in front of him.

"Why would you say that, honey?"

"You don't look right."

"I look perfectly fine. Of course I'm your mum."

"Prove it!"

"Will you please stop shouting and eat your breakfast."

"Show me your teeth. If you're my mum, you'll show me your teeth."

She scowled and opened her mouth wide. Nigel shook his head.

"Nope, mummy's teeth are pointed. Show me your tail."

"What?

"I said, show me your tail!"

It was then the shape shifter realised they'd picked the wrong house to infiltrate.

## What Are Little Girls Made Of?

Her spine prickled like a thousand needles were bursting through her flesh.

Taut skin split, peeling away from her growing frame. She writhed beneath her sweat-drenched duvet, legs tangled in bloody sheets.

Thick fur sprouted between her tatters of creamy skin.

Gelatinous gore clung to the walls and floor; her soft toys had absorbed the rest.

Wolf-girl crawled out of bed and clawed at the locked door; grounded for coming home late from trick or treating.

They hadn't seen her bloodstained legs, or the bite.

They wouldn't ground this beast again, if they tried, they'd get a fright.

## The Wailing

The wailing never stops, never lets up.

It's a cat with its balls caught in a car door, it's donald trump* trying to say the word "anonymous."

Whenever Millie shuts her eyes, it gets louder - she can't escape.

Her ears, plugged with globs of super glue. Frustrated sobs wrack her frame, her forehead a puckered crater from repeatedly bashing it against the bare bricks above her useless bed.

Grasping pens in her fists, she drives the ballpoints into her ears, her shrieks drowning in the molten blast of agony.

A fraction of blessed calm follows, but then, the wailing continues.

*He doesn't deserve capitalisation.

## The Last Crop

Atop Gallows hill, my quivering hand grips Shelley's as we watch the molten harvest sun sink below the horizon.

Before we descend, I say farewell to the light.

The others stand in a rigid circle, each desperately clinging to their turnip lantern.

Through tears, Shelley helps me from my clothing. I don't fight as another binds my hands. I do this for her, I remind myself, as the frigid stone altar makes my naked flesh clench.

The creature grumbles from the dark.

I buy her one year. A single cycle of plenty. Next harvest, it will be her turn.

## Hell

Hunched, he stepped slowly through the delicate veil of white. Hot air stifled shallow breaths, burned lips, and marred flesh.

A light of fulfilment, of peace, was promised to him, not an oil slick spiral staircase of decay and descent. Plumes of ash danced in shimmering waves of heat which coiled between flame-lined cracks in worn stone steps.

Grotesque drumming signalled his entrance into the depths, the thunderous sound of meatless bone striking taut flayed skins, tortured screams from ember scarred lips the welcoming fanfare. Delicate gold letters adorned an arched doorway: *Abandon all hope, ye who enter here.*

## Always Keep the Lanterns Lit

Keep your pumpkins lit from dusk till dawn,
to keep the Eaters at bay.
They live in spaces between the things you see;
where blind, they shriek, and play.
When they are near, you will know their scent,
it's honey, jam, and fresh baked bread.
You will not see them with your eyes, and your skin will shrink around your frame,
when they'll slither beneath your bed.
So close your eyes,
pull the blanket up over your head.
But, if the pumpkins go out, they will bare their teeth, and then, my boy, you will wish that you were dead.

## Last Call

Casey's night had been lunacy, but that's Halloween.

The patrons had him in stitches with their costumes: sultry vampires, a politician with an orange face and bleached anus eyes. There was even a couple dressed as a pair of enormous tits. Lefty had spent her night propping up righty, who'd started drooping after a single Jaeger.

*

After Casey locked up, he noticed a horned man sitting at the bar.

The man started to speak but Casey cut him off — "Fuck off, like I told you before, there's nothing in the world I'd be dumb enough to swap my soul for."

## Whispers From Beneath

"Shesa?"

"Yes, my little one?" A voice from beneath the bed seemed to vibrate Jason's mattress.

"Will you still be with me when I'm growed up?"

There was a moment of silence, made longer by the stillness of the night. Then, the thing under the bed let out a thundering sigh.

Jason felt something slither up the end of the bed beneath the blankets, until it caressed his hand.

It felt the way Jason had always imagined tarantulas he'd seen might feel, but he didn't flinch.

"I'll love you always," Shesa said. "I would follow you until the end of the world."

## Sounds Like Supper

I love the melodic notes of their screams from my basement, my little choir of snotty noses and tear-streaked faces.

I pluck them off the street one-by-one, ushering them in my front door for more treats. I like the fat ones with rotund tummies beneath their grotesque costumes; extra meat for the pot.

Two or three kids can last me all year.

I let them sing for a while, and enjoy my private symphony. But the stew won't make itself.

I love bursting in as they reach the chorus, and cutting them off a note early.

"Surprise! It's supper time."

## Not Twice, Randy Brindle.

If ever a child needed his arse smacked raw - it was Randy Brindle.

He'd TP'd the church, destroyed the Coffee Bean bathroom with cherry-bombs, and sugared Principal Gibbon's engine.

But crossing Haggie Johns was the last straw.

He smashed every pot plat on her porch before grabbing the biggest Jack o' lantern.

But the gourd's jaws clamped down on his wrist and engulfed his arm up to the elbow in milliseconds; bones crunching, he didn't even have time to scream.

Through the darkened window, Haggie watched the legs disappear down its chomping gullet.

Grinning, she popped the kettle on.

## Firedance

The naked women prancing around the flames are anything but slender and lithe. Their wrinkled sagging breasts flap like old leather in a tempest.

They chant, callous voices echoing through the hollow. They call to the nefarious things on the other side of the veil; things that creep and slurp. They promise them delights of pleasure and moist flesh.

Sometimes, the demons attend, sharing their secret wisdoms whilst they bed the witches down on the frigid grass.

But when the beasts do not come, the aged crones wrap themselves in homemade blankets and knit itchy jumpers for their in-laws.

## Halloween

Fire crackles between decomposing leaves, orange flames that signal summer's end.

Samhain is here, and the seasons must change.

It's their time, and the Unseelie court demands it.

The musty perfume of decay ushers in mischievous fae, for tricks and treats.

Whispers on the wind say, *wrap up warm my children, the dark is here and All Hallows Eve is soon to follow.*

Keep your lamps lit, and bolt your doors. For the things that crawl and snap will roam again.

Carve your faces and protect your homes; the boundary is broken, and the living and dead walk as one.

# POISONED CANDY

## BITE-SIZED HORROR

# WHICH STORY MADE YOU CRINGE, LAUGH, OR SHAKE YOUR HEAD?

We'd love to hear what you thought of Poisoned Candy.

Leaving reviews is one of the best ways you can support independent creators, and more importantly, without your help we're limited to who we can offend, and that's just not good enough.

## PLEASE LEAVE A REVIEW

on Amazon, Goodreads, Barnes & Noble, Kobo, or wherever you purchased this book!

## OR YOU CAN

email us directly, to give us a piece of your mind
**pugnaciouspress@gmail.com**

## BUT IF YOU LOVED THIS BOOK

you should definitely check out our Patreon where you can get your hands on exclusive goodies like story workshops, access to author's notebooks, behind the scenes video, and all sorts of exclusive content.

**www.patreon.com/pugnaciouspress**

RANCID EGGS
BITE-SIZED HORROR
PIPPA BAILEY & MYK PILGRIM

DEVIL'S NIGHT
BITE-SIZED HORROR
PIPPA BAILEY & MYK PILGRIM

BLOODY STOCKINGS
BITE-SIZED HORROR
PIPPA BAILEY & MYK PILGRIM

THE LITTLE BOOK OF
HARM
VERONICA ABBOTT

A SZIMPLA
ÖRÖMET OKOZHAT!
THE DIVE

# PUGNACIOUS PRESS

This book was created with the fine contributions of our excellent Patrons.

**J.W. Donely**

**Katie Whittle**

**Mark Young**

**Nelson W. Pyles**

If you would also like to get access to years and years of private notebooks from our indentured authors, listen in on story brainstorming sessions, behind the scenes video diaries, research notes, get copies of books in advance of public release AND see your name in print –

Then you need to haul ass over to the Pugnacious Press Patreon page at

**www.patreon.com/pugnaciouspress**

and be blown away by how much awesome you can get for one measly dollar a month.

## PIPPA BAILEY

Pippa Bailey lives north of the wall in the Scottish Highlands. Principally a horror writer with Pugnacious Press Publishing, and YouTube personality and independent reviewer at Deadflicks with her husband, Myk Pilgrim.

Pippa's work has appeared alongside Clive Barker, Ramsey Campbell, Jack Ketchum, Joe R Lansdale, and the marvelous Myk Pilgrim in Dark Faces Evil Place 2.

Her stories have been published in 13 Wicked Tales; a Wicked Library Anthology, featured on the Wicked Library podcast, Frisson Comics, Sirens Call Magazine, & Holiday-themed horror collections with Myk Pilgrim.

You can spot her drinking too much tea, making terrible puns, and bothering the local wildlife.

## Acknowledgements Pippa

I would like to thank Nelson Pyles, for his ongoing support with everything I've done, whether that be my stories, or my social media endeavours.

To my parents, I know you don't really understand the journey I'm on, and that's OK. But, thank you for letting me just be me.

I also want to thank Kitty Kane, Matty-Bob Cash, Em Dehaney and Lisa-Lee Tone for helping me become a better author and a better person.

James Kiernan, for listening to my random ideas for the last year.

Tara & David Court - Tara, thanks for threatening Myk; he's so scared, he's stuck around for almost a year!

Theresa Derwin, Dave Robison, Rick Powell, Katie Whittle of Frisson comics, and the rest of the people I share my crap with on Facebook. You're all awesome, and fill me to the brim with ideas on a daily basis.

Myk, I couldn't have done this without you, mostly because you can art and I make stick men look bad. Honestly, you're my rock, and my everything, thank you for letting me into your crazy world and helping us build one together.

## MYK PILGRIM

Myk Pilgrim is a horror writer, or at least that's what he likes to tell people.

He lives in a town north of the wall, where he spends his time sharing cappuccinos with his inner demons, binge-watching horror movies with his equally demented writing partner & wife Pippa Bailey, shaving his head, annoying the locals, and generally counting down the days until Halloween.

Also, sometimes, when he's not too busy flaunting his Best Legs in Horror 2019 status, he writes stuff.

Myk's work has appeared alongside Clive Barker, Ramsey Campbell, & Jack Ketchum in Dark Faces Evil Place 2. His stories have featured in 13 Wicked Tales; a Wicked Library Anthology, featured on their podcast, in Frisson Comics, Sirens Call Magazine, & Holiday-themed horror collections with Pippa Bailey

## Acknowledgements Myk

I'd like to thank Joanna "Melfka" Maciejewska, JR Bee, & Lucy Jayne for their unflappable support, friendship, and painful honesty over the last five years. I would not have survived 2017 without you. Even when I'm silent online, you're all in my thoughts.

Thank you to Christie Stratos, JD "If King Kong & Godzilla made the sex, who'd be on top?" Estrada, Dave Robison of the Archivos Podcast – Sir, you've been there helping me long before you ever knew I was digging through your trashcans in the middle of the night, Ian "sexy voice" Newton from Something Vloggy, Clara Bush, Joshua Robertson & Lilian Oake, Joe McMahon, Joe Compton, Nelson W Pyles, Rick Powell, Amber Sayge, Laura Matheson
- if you're on this list, you'll know what you did.

Pippa you beautiful, wonderful, sick fuck, thank you for everything - you make my universe feel like Halloween every single day. I could not imagine my life without you holding my hand.

Hungry for more Bite-sized Horror?

Here's a **FREE** preview of

# RANCID EGGS

that you can stick up your chocolate hole right now!

# WELCOME TO RANCID EGGS

At the point of this writing, Pip and I are sitting in the window of one of our favourite local cafes. Our backs are warmer than either of us have been in months, and goddamn does it feel like there might be an end to winter at long fucking last.It feels like hope, and with the state of the world right now (Feb 2nd, 2019), I think we could all use a little hope.

People are greater than we give ourselves credit for, though it may not feel like it sometimes. When it comes down to the wire, any person with a soul will shove that Westboro Baptist down a flight of stairs.

They will vote to have that anus-eyed, septic tank in a red hat disqualified from the human race.

Hell, sometimes they might even hold the door open for you when you've got your arms full of shopping.

Humans will surprise you, they are funny like that.

So, however you're planning on celebrating the end of winter, be it joining an Easter-themed bunny-tailed orgy, a ritual burning of believers in a giant wicker man, or just smearing your genitals in chocolate and hoping your significant other isn't too committed to their chocolate-free lent, we wish you all the best for the season and pretty much life in general (unless, of course, your name is donald trump).

But seriously though, there is a lot of bonking in this book, so consider yourself warned. Enjoy!

*Myk Pilgrim*
*Scotland, April 2019*

RANCID
EGGS
BITE-SIZED HORROR
PIPPA BAILEY & MYK PILGRIM

# The Woodend Village Annual Egg Roll

Only the worst children get the honour. The parents of the village get their votes in, and when the drawing comes through on Good Friday, there are more tears of joy than anyone might believe.

The following night, the elders waste no time in snatching the chosen "eggs" from their beds and, with their parent's blessing, drag them screaming to the catacombs under the village church.

Where the preparations start.

The children are soaked in warm, salted water for three minutes exactly. Then they are held down and have ALL their hair shaved off. One might be inclined to think this is hardest on the girls, but if anyone is most likely to wail like a little girl with a skinned knee, it's the boys.

After that, they are dunked in dye baths, which shade them any one of a million striking rainbow colours.

On Easter Sunday, hands and feet bound, the naked children are carried to the peak of Monument Hill, where the fun really starts.

The entire village assembles on the hillside. The festive drinking starts early of course, so the whooping and cheering is particularly merry.

Elected representatives from all five counties stand behind their hogtied charges and, at the mark, kick the struggling eggs down the hill with all their might.

And the race is off, the rainbow coloured bodies roll down the hill like so many billiard balls. Unable to halt their tumble, or direct their spinning bodies, the human eggs plough through the low brush. They hurtle through bushes, disturbing birds and picking up all kinds of thorns.

If any become lodged and stop rolling, an Egg Marshall will lift them from the ditch and send them back on their way.

The first egg over the finish line wins nothing, as does the second, the third, fourth, and fifth.

Though if all is as it should be, and the naughty little bastards have in fact learnt their lesson, they will never misbehave again. Woodend is renowned the world over for having the best-behaved children, and if that isn't considered first prize for any community, I don't know what is.

## Following the Trail

Scouring the ground, the bush, and the pond, sticky little fingers raked past the coloured orbs hidden in nooks and crannies. The wandering children blindly followed trails into darkened places, lighting them with their laughter.

Like the Pied-Piper, chocolate Easter eggs guided a stream of children towards his house; the old man on the corner, with his blacked-out windows and rotten fence posts. “Stay away from number 13,” their parents would say. But who can deny a child’s whimsy when faced with the promise of more sweets and treats?

Number 13 had waited all year for this moment, prepared and planned his Easter hunt. He’d filled the eggs with enough sedative to ensure they wouldn’t fight back—he wasn’t as strong as he used to be. He smiled, reminiscing on decades of gripping his fleshy, squealing quarry before sinking his teeth into them—happy memories. At least now he didn’t have to hunt. They would come to him.

One by one they clambered through his back door and into his kitchen, sluggishly pushing each other out of the way grappling for the last few eggs, chocolaty fingers slipping on the shiny wrappers. Yawning, they hunted through cupboards, on chairs, and under tables, while several collapsed onto the dirty linoleum floor.

They were so distracted, they didn’t notice the back door click shut, or the man in the dirty bunny suit hop into view—adjusting his eggs.

## The Church of the Perpetually Stiff Bunny

They came from all over the globe. Flying cross-country from Utah. Taking the long haul in from Sydney via Thailand. Afrikaners and Zulus fly in from Jo'burg. Excited conversations in Mandarin and broken Russian-English echo through the hallways of the hotel lobby.

Which, in even an age of impossibilities, manages to enforce its will on the convention centre. The attendees mostly know not to bring cameras, or video cameras—for the most obvious reason.

As by design, smart-phones within the bounds of the cordoned off convention centre stop working. As a side effect, electronics like TVs and radios also fizzle if one was to try to turn them on, but no-one has come all this way to sit on their ass and watch other people live their lives—well, not over a screen anyway.

All music within the area is provided by actual instruments, but on request, the organisers will have a vintage gramophone sent to your room.

The hotel never belongs to the church, but for security, they staff it themselves, pulling from a massive pool of blind workers from all over the world. No-one on the outside should ever see anything that goes on, much less speak of it.

When the day of the Feast arrives, the outfits are numerous. Full-body furry style bunny and hare suits with animatronic facial features and open mouths for convenient tongue to genital access. Others as simple as bare skin with fluffy rabbit butt-plugs and bunny-eared Alice-bands. Some wear rabbit skin thongs with a kaleidoscope of spring flowers in their hair.

Lifelong cosplayers would have much to learn from their practicality. The furry suits have zippers in all conceivable places for access and easy to reach pockets stuffed with wet wipes and lube. But there are no contraceptives, that would be counterproductive for the church's aims.

They crowd into yiffing piles on the painted wooden floor, which was installed specially for this and only this occasion. Searching fingers extract snorts and whines as any and all exchange fluids. The room's energy increases with the funk of sweating bodies beneath the sex-soaked fur, waves of urgency driving them onwards.

Some of the older attendees have to stop, struggling for breath, grasping their chests. They can't keep up like they used to and sit it out to admire the hedonistic spectacle of the youth at play.

They reminisce with lifelong friends until they get their second wind and return to the fray as rigid a boy scout in a strip club.

As the orgy climbs towards its peak, tendrils of dark energy slither from the edges of the room and dispense their own pleasures on the assembled devout. The unpronounceable symbols etched into the floor ignite, bathing the pile of naked, writhing flesh in a lurid lilac glow. When the torrent of orgasms begins, the foundations beneath them quake hard enough to make the crystal chandeliers swing in a violent trapeze.

And with that, the deed is done.

The following day they part, nameless, exhausted, and satisfied, and return to their normal lives, which by comparison are benign.

The women pray that they may be the one who gifts queen Shub-Niggurath with a body. The men, however, can only seethe in envy at their inability to garner such favour.

# Sentient Eggs!

**Are you bored of your usual anti-wank flake or nugget-based breakfast? Need more murder in your morning?**

**Start your day right with Sentient Eggs!**
**These hairless, defenceless critters aren't just tasty and nutritious. Owing to our not quite yet patented limbless body technology, the little fellows can't run away when you come at them with your teaspoon.**

**What is more, Sentient Eggs feel actual pain and cry real tears! They shriek like a feline with its nuts trapped in a car door when you strike 'em to get at the wonderful deliciousness inside!**

## Imagine people you hate as you smash open Sentient Eggs!

**Your boss, your Ex, that teacher who picked on you in pre-school, that annoying relative who always guilts you about your lack of marital status, your creepy Uncle Nelson, my creepy Uncle Nelson, your mother-in-law, bigots, or even just that barista who keeps spelling your name wrong.**

78 out of 100 convicted felons swear that Sentient Eggs have kept them well-fed during particularly long murder sprees
100% naturally grown in organically sourced test tubes in a lab that totally has a tree growing somewhere nearby!
100% of Vegans will not endorse Sentient Eggs!

## Plugged Up

June adjusted her nipple clamps and positioned herself behind Keith. Pegging was new to both of them, but Sex-dungeon Steve had recommended it as something all the kids were doing nowadays.

Keith was always up for a new challenge, although he'd only recently worked out how to use his grandson's fidget spinner, so this was going to be quite a game changer.

Steve peered into the room, a bottle of lube and two love-eggs on a connected rubber string dangling from his hand. "How are you two getting on?" he smiled. "Thought I'd pop these in here." He snickered at his own joke. "Free of charge, of course, part of the Easter deal."

June gave him a thumbs up and smiled.

Keith gritted his teeth on his ball-gag creating what looked more like a grimace than a smile. Not trusting his arthritic wrists, he didn't bring his hands up from the squishy floor mat.

Steve popped the freebies onto a side table and swung the door shut. "Well, you crazy kids have fun!" he shouted with a thick Yorkshire accent through the thin wooden door. It left a lot to be desired dungeon wise, but it was a 1970s house, and Steve had worked with what he had at the time.

June squirted a palm full of lube and applied it to Keith's salt and pepper starfish, the cold making it pucker.

She leaned in close and whispered into his ear, "The safety word is Garibaldi."

Other than a few issues with June's hip and Keith's knee, their first foray into the world of BDSM fun had gone without a hitch. Next on the agenda was to try those love-eggs Steve had popped in the door. They didn't look too dangerous. June pulled a tab out of the side of the smooth pink plastic, and they set off vibrating in her hand like an angry bee.

"Oh, lover?"

She ran her hand across Keith's back and withdrew her plastic schlong from his bruised rectum.

"Yeths, Mwithgwess," he mumbled through his gag.

"Ready for something else new?"

He nodded.

She ran her fingers around his crimson sphincter and slipped the first egg in. It disappeared with a pop, tugging on the string and slamming the second orb against him. Keith moaned.

"Oh, honey, that sounded like my hip when I'm walking down the stairs."

He nodded again.

"More?"

"Yeths, Mwithgwess."

She slipped the second vibrating egg into him.

It vanished like a bullet train through the darkness, or in Keith's case to where the sun doesn't shine.

June, very much in the moment, slipped a finger in too, chasing after the remnants of the latter love-egg.

"You enjoying that?"

Keith grimaced but nodded.

She probed in further, finger now only touching his squishy insides.

"Gawebawldee" Keith murmured.

"Okay, time to take them out."

He nodded.

"Right, oh, I'm not too sure how to do that. Can you push?"

Keith bared down, producing nothing but a careless whisper of gas.

June slipped the ball gag out of his mouth. "It doesn't feel good," he said, rubbing his stomach.

"I'll see if I can get it, push again."

She slipped a finger back into him. "I can't get it. Hold on, I'll find something to help."

Siding out of the door, June headed down the hallway to what was a drink and snack bar. She yanked a pair of tongs out of the ice and headed back to Keith, who was laying on his side.

"I've got you, lover."

She spread his cheeks and slipped the tongs into his ass, attempting to open him wide and get to her pink vibrating prize … she was less than successful.

After about twenty minutes of prodding and poking and lubing and pushing, the vibrating eggs still hadn't made an appearance.

"I don't think it's working." Keith clambered up from the floor and leaned against a bondage bench for support. "Let's go home. I'm sure I can squeeze them out by tonight."

*

When Keith arrived at A&E three days later, having not 'squeezed out' the love eggs, he was looking a little green. A few hours of concentrated squatting over their magnolia bidet had only led to pelvic pain. June had taken it upon herself to D.I.Y. a way out of the situation. Unfortunately for Keith, that included using a speculum, a wire coat-hanger, and copious amounts of super glue. All attempts had been less than successful, one probe piercing his intestinal wall and hooking around a length of bowel. This was yet another surprise for the doctor who attempted to diagnose Keith's condition.

It's amazing the shit people do in the name of love.

RANCID
EGGS
BITE-SIZED HORROR
PIPPA BAILEY & MYK PILGRIM

RANCID EGGS
BITE-SIZED HORROR
PIPPA BAILEY & MYK PILGRIM

DEVIL'S NIGHT
BITE-SIZED HORROR
PIPPA BAILEY & MYK PILGRIM

BLOODY STOCKINGS
BITE-SIZED HORROR
PIPPA BAILEY & MYK PILGRIM

THE LITTLE BOOK OF
HARM
VERONICA ABBOTT

DEVIL'S NIGHT
BITE-SIZED HORROR
PIPPA BAILEY & MYK PILGRIM

BLOODY STOCKINGS
BITE-SIZED HORROR
PIPPA BAILEY & MYK PILGRIM

THE LITTLE BOOK OF
HARM
VERONICA ABBOTT

Happy

lloween!
om Myk & Pippa!

# LINKS

Get Free Books and instant access to author's notebooks, story workshops, behind the scenes video, and all sorts of exclusive content by joining the Puggle horde at

www.patreon.com/PugnaciousPress

Myk Pilgrim

WEBSITE: www.mykpilgrim.com

INSTAGRAM: www.instagram.com/mykpilgrimauthor

FACEBOOK: www.facebook.com/mykpilgrim

TWITTER: www.twitter.com/mykpilgrim

Pippa Bailey

WEBSITE: www.pippabailey.co.uk

INSTAGRAM: www.instagram.com/pippabaileyauthor

FACEBOOK: www.facebook.com/PippaBaileyauthor

TWITTER: www.twitter.com/ThePippaBailey

Pugnacious Press

WEBSITE: www.PugnaciousPress.com

INSTAGRAM: www.instagram.com/PugnaciousPress

FACEBOOK: www.facebook.com/PugnaciousPress

TWITTER: www.twitter.com/PugnaciousPress

MAIL: PugnaciousPress@gmail.com

Milton Keynes UK
Ingram Content Group UK Ltd.
UKHW040852050124
435493UK00005B/752

9 781393 878452